D1135311

ty Library

Withdrawn Stock

Class No. _____ J/5-8 Acc No. C141739

Author: AHLBERG, A   Loc: 5 MAY 1993

LEABHARLANN
CHONDAE AN CHABHAIN

_____

_____

_____

1. **This book may be kept three weeks. It is to be
   returned on / before the last date stamped below.**
2. **A fine of 20p will**
   part of week a boo

2 5 JUN 1993   2 1 OCT 1994
   9 JUL 1993
   4 AUG 1993   2 3 DEC 1994
1 0 NOV 1993   1 7 MAR 1995
   1 1 NOV 1993   1 SEP 1995
   1 0 DEC 1993   0 NOV 1995
2 9 JAN 1994   1 2 MAR 1997
   2 1 APR 1994   2 6 MAR 1997
      2 9 APR 1994   27 JUN 1997
1 5 JUN 1994   1 3 JAN 1999
         2 0 FEB 1999

Master Salt the Sailors' Son

by ALLAN AHLBERG

with pictures by
ANDRE AMSTUTZ

Puffin

Viking

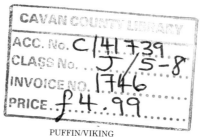

CAVAN COUNTY LIBRARY
ACC. No. C/4739
CLASS No. J/5-8
INVOICE NO. 1746
PRICE £4.99

PUFFIN/VIKING

Published by the Penguin Group
Penguin Books Ltd, 27 Wrights Lane, London W8 5TZ, England
Viking Penguin, a division of Penguin Books USA Inc.
375 Hudson Street, New York, New York 10014, USA
Penguin Books Australia Ltd, Ringwood, Victoria, Australia
Penguin Books Canada Ltd, 2801 John Street, Markham, Ontario, Canada L3R 1B4
Penguin Books (NZ) Ltd, 182–190 Wairau Road, Auckland 10, New Zealand

Penguin Books Ltd, Registered Offices: Harmondsworth, Middlesex, England

First published 1980
5 7 9 10 8 6

Text copyright © Allan Ahlberg, 1980
Illustrations copyright © Joe Wright, 1980

Educational Advisory Editor: Brian Thompson

All rights reserved
Without limiting the rights under copyright
reserved above, no part of this publication may be
reproduced, stored in or introduced into a retrieval system,
or transmitted, in any form or by any means (electronic, mechanical,
photocopying, recording or otherwise), without the prior
written permission of both the copyright owner and
the above publisher of this book

Printed and bound in Great Britain by
William Clowes Limited, Beccles and London
Set in Century Schoolbook by Filmtype Services Limited, Scarborough

ISBN Paperback 0 14 03.1237 4
ISBN Hardback 0-670-80575-0

Mr Salt the sailor sailed the seven seas.
Mrs Salt sailed the seven seas as well.
So did Miss Salt.
Master Salt did not sail the seas.
He was too little.
He stayed on shore with his grandpa.

One day exciting things happened.
Mr and Mrs Salt got ready for a voyage.
"We are going to sail to
Coconut Island," they said.
Their ship was called the *Jolly Jack*.

Mr Salt cleaned the cabins
and washed the deck.
Mrs Salt and Sally Salt painted the funnel.
Sammy Salt sulked.
He wanted to go on a voyage too.

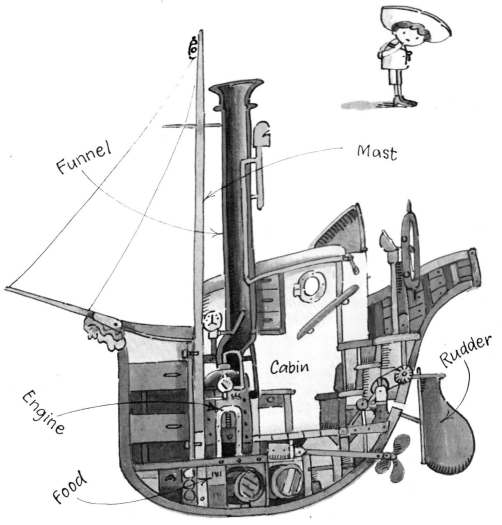

Funnel

Mast

Cabin

Rudder

Engine

Food

The next day the *Jolly Jack*
was ready to sail.
Mr and Mrs Salt pulled up the anchor.
Grandpa Salt stood on the shore.
But where was Sammy Salt?

The *Jolly Jack* sailed out to sea.
Sally Salt blew a kiss to her grandpa.
He waved goodbye from the shore.
But *where* was Sammy Salt?

The voyage began.
The *Jolly Jack* sailed past a lighthouse.
Sally Salt got the dinner ready.
Somebody's little hand reached out.
"Who's been eating *my* fish?" said Mr Salt.

The *Jolly Jack* sailed past
a big ship.

Mr Salt got the tea ready.
Somebody's little hand reached out again.
"Who's been eating *my* boiled egg?"
said Mrs Salt.

The *Jolly Jack* sailed past a whale.
Mrs Salt got the supper ready.
Somebody's little hand reached out again!
"Who's been drinking *my* cocoa?"
said Sally Salt.

In the night strange things happened.
Sally Salt woke up.
She said her nose kept tickling.
"Don't be silly, Sally," said Mr Salt.
Then Mr Salt went to bed and *he* woke up.
"My nose keeps tickling," he said.

In the morning more strange things happened.
Somebody's little footprints appeared on deck.
Somebody's little teeth-marks
appeared in an apple.
When Mr Salt was fishing,
somebody's little boot appeared
on the end of his line.

Then, in the afternoon,
terrible things happened.
There was a storm.
The rain fell and the wind blew.
The thunder thundered and
the lightning flashed.
The *Jolly Jack* tipped up and down
– and Mr Salt fell overboard!
"Man overboard!" shouted Mr Salt.

Mrs Salt came to the rescue.
But still the *Jolly Jack* tipped up
and down – and *she* fell overboard!
"Woman overboard!" shouted Mrs Salt.
Sally Salt came to the rescue.
But still the *Jolly Jack* tipped up
and down – and *she* fell overboard!
"Girl overboard!" shouted Sally Salt.

The next minute surprising things happened.
Somebody appeared on deck.
He threw a rope to Mr Salt.
"That's clever!" said Mr Salt.
He threw a lifebelt to Mrs Salt.
"Just what I need!" Mrs Salt said.
He threw a rubber-ring to Sally Salt.
She did not say a word.
He rescued them all!

"What a surprise!" said Mrs Salt.
"Look who it is!" said Mr Salt.
"It's Sammy!" said Sally.
Sammy Salt made hot drinks for
his family.
He wrapped them up in blankets.
He steered the ship.

"Now I know who tickled my nose,"
said Mr Salt.
"And drank my cocoa," said Sally Salt.
"And ate my boiled egg!" Mrs Salt said.
"That's right," said Sammy Salt. "It was me!"

After that the best things happened.
The storm blew away.
The *Jolly Jack* reached
Coconut Island.

There was a picnic on the shore,
and paddling in the sea,
and hide-and-seek in the jungle.

Bedtime came.
Mr and Mrs Salt and the children
slept out under the stars.
Then, in the night,
the last thing happened.
Sammy Salt woke up.
"My nose keeps tickling," he said.

CAVAN COUNTY LIBRARY

The End